D0188908

MO'S MISCHIEF

Super Cool Uncle

Other titles in the Mo's Mischief series:

MO'S MISCHIEF

Super Cool Uncle

Hongying Yang

HarperCollins *Children's Books*

First published in China by Jieli Publishing House 2004
First published in Great Britain by HarperCollins *Children's Books* 2008
HarperCollins *Children's Books* is a division of HarperCollins*Publishers* Ltd
77-85 Fulham Palace Road, Hammersmith, London W6 8JB

The HarperCollins *Children's Books* website address is
www.harpercollinschildrensbooks.co.uk

1

Text copyright © Hongying Yang 2004
English translation © HarperCollins Publishers 2008

Illustrations © Pencil Tip Culture & Art Co 2004

Hongying Yang asserts the moral right to be identified
as the author of this work

ISBN 978-0-00-728432-0

Printed and bound in England by
Clays Ltd, St Ives plc

Conditions of Sale
This book is sold subject to the condition that it shall not, by way of trade or
otherwise, be lent, re-sold, hired out or otherwise circulated without the
publisher's prior written consent in any form of binding or cover other than
that in which it is published and without a similar condition including
this condition being imposed on the subsequent purchaser.

GLASGOW CITY COUNCIL	
LIBRARIES INFORMATION & LEARNING	
C004126933	
EA	PETERS
05-Aug-2008	£4.99
JF	

A BRAND NEW HUMAN

Mo's mother had a brother and his name was Dink. Mo thought his uncle was the coolest person he had ever met. Uncle Dink had been to university in Shanghai and then moved on to Beijing, where he was a whizkid with computers. He'd then moved to different cities in China for work, but now he was coming home.

Mo hadn't seen his uncle for years but he'd heard his parents and their friends calling Uncle Dink a 'brand new human'.

"Dad, what's the difference between brand new humans and humans like us?"

Mo and his father, Mr Ma, were on their way to the airport to meet Uncle Dink.

"Brand new humans are quite different from us, Mo. They work hard but they also play hard; they don't mind what people think about them and they like to be noticed. When you meet Uncle Dink, you'll know what I mean!"

To Mo, Uncle Dink was as mysterious as the abominable snowman and he couldn't wait to meet him.

"What does Uncle Dink do?"

"He's a computer software engineer. A very clever business man who will make lots of money."

Mo immediately formed a picture of Uncle Dink in his mind: a smart haircut, polished black shoes, a sharp single-breasted jacket with two buttons or an equally sharp double-breasted jacket with four buttons, a pure-silk tie which was heavy and thick, and a big shiny briefcase.

When they arrived at the airport they saw from the board that Uncle Dink's flight had arrived.

Many smart business men and women walked into the arrivals hall, dragging their suitcases behind them, but there was no sign of Uncle Dink.

"Do you think we've met the right flight?" Mo asked anxiously.

"I think so," said Mr Ma, taking out a small piece of paper from his jacket pocket: "Flight 4107. That's right."

Mo had made a card on which was written "Welcome Home Uncle Dink". Mo's handwriting was quite poor, especially when using big felt pens, but he had managed to write the words nice and big.

Mo held the card up high – he was afraid that Uncle Dink would sneak away and get a taxi.

Then a young man with rainbow-coloured hair, tight leather jeans and a leather jacket covered in studs and zippers walked straight towards Mo. He stopped in front of the board, craned his neck to one side, and tried very hard not to laugh.

"Hi, Dink!" Even Mr Ma had great difficulty in recognising his wife's brother.

"Brother-in-law!" said the man. Then he pointed at Mo. "Is this little Mo, your precious only son?"

"Who else could he be?" said Mr Ma. He looked around. "Where's your luggage?"

"This is it."

Mo could see that Uncle Dink was only carrying a

laptop in one hand and a mobile in the other. Uncle Dink said, "See here, a laptop, a mobile, a credit card and passport. It's enough for me to travel around the world and live a happy life."

Uncle Dink held Mo's hand and strode off towards the car park. He had such long legs that Mo had to scamper to keep up with him.

Mr Ma drove Uncle Dink to his parents' house. During the ride, Mo couldn't stop staring at Uncle Dink. He looked more like a pop star than a businessman!

Like Mr Ma, Grandpa and Grandma had not seen Uncle Dink for two or three years. His colourful hair alone was enough to make them almost faint.

"Oh no, Dink," said Grandma. "Someone has dropped paint on your head!"

Mo's Grandma tried to persuade Uncle Dink to wash the paint off his hair. Uncle Dink found it both funny and annoying.

"Don't be silly!" said Mo. "That's not paint. Uncle Dink *chose* to have his hair dyed like that."

Grandpa and Grandma remained confused. "Why would he do that?"

Mr Ma, worrying about more squabbling, suggested that Dink might be tired from his flight and want to freshen up in his room.

"Oh, I'm not staying here," Uncle Dink explained. "The company have rented a flat for me."

"Ridiculous!" said Grandpa. "We have plenty of rooms but you would rather stay outside in a rented house, it doesn't make sense."

Grandma was upset too. "You wicked son. We have kept all your things unchanged in your room, even though you have been away for years. Your room is just as usual, and your guitar, your tennis racket are still in the same place…nothing has been changed…"

Grandma got angrier when she spoke and Uncle Dink felt a bit guilty. He put his arm around his mother to comfort her.

Mo realised that Grandpa and Grandma still had no idea that Uncle Dink had become a brand new human. That was why they couldn't understand his weird behaviour. But Mo could. How could someone be a brand new human if he hadn't changed at all?

"Grandpa and Grandma, I'm afraid there is one thing you still don't know – Uncle Dink has become a brand new human!"

"What's a brand new human? An alien?" Grandma asked. "I gave birth to this boy – how could he turn into an alien?"

Grandma grabbed Uncle Dink's arm. "Did you get abducted by aliens and forced to become an alien too?"

Grandma had seen something about UFOs in the newspapers and on TV. She was quite old, but she had a good imagination, thought Mo.

Uncle Dink gave up. He knew he would never be able to persuade his parents that he was a modern man and that he didn't live in the dark ages like they did. Mr Ma drove him to an apartment block in the city where he would be living. The flat was on the twenty-ninth floor and Mo was longing to see inside it, but his dad wanted to get home.

When he said goodbye, Uncle Dink gave Mo an unexpected smile. Mo took this to be a good sign. Uncle Dink liked him!

FINDING OUT

Mo became more and more fascinated by Uncle Dink, but Grandpa and Grandma were more and more annoyed by him. Next time he visited them, they asked where his office was. He said anywhere and everywhere. When they asked how long his working hours were, he said as long or as little as it took.

"Son-in-law," they said to Mo's dad. "You are the director of a toy factory, you should discipline your brother-in-law a little bit!"

Mr Ma knew what he could do and what he could not do. Disciplining a brand new human like Uncle

Dink was not possible. How can you discipline a person when you don't even know what that person does all day long?

Mo's grandparents' hope lay in Mo. They thought their grandson was the cleverest and most precious boy in the world. They also knew how curious he was about everything. They would send him to find out what his brand-new-human uncle was up to!

First they went to the supermarket to buy Mo's favourite snacks.

They carried a big bag of food and went to meet Mo after school.

Mo was absolutely starving – he'd had a very busy day being mischievous at school. He tore open a bag of crisps and began to eat. He crunched and munched as he listened to his Grandma and then his Grandpa. Finally he put his hand on his heart and promised to do his best and find out what Uncle Dink did.

Grandpa and Grandma decided that it was worth buying all that food for Mo, and so did someone else.

"Mo!" a voice shouted.

"Mo! Wait for us," cried two more voices.

It was Penguin, Monkey and Hippo, Mo's best friends. He thought they had gone home, but they could see the bag of food and decided to wait for Mo.

"Mo, what's in that supermarket bag?"

They already knew it was full of food...

Mo said nothing.

"Mo, are we still good friends?" Penguin said, loudly. "Because good friends share everything..."

Now Penguin never liked to share anything with his friends, and certainly not food. But Mo was a kind and generous boy and he had an idea! He took out three bags of crisps, and gave one to each of his three friends.

While they were munching, Mo said, "I have a question for you guys. A man does not go to work everyday, but he earns a lot of money. What does he do?"

"Is this some kind of riddle, Mo? Or are you talking about someone in particular?" asked Monkey.

"I am talking about my Uncle Dink," replied Mo.

"Well, he must be a professional hit man," said Monkey, quick as a flash.

Mo didn't like Monkey's answer.

"He must be a gambler," said Penguin.

Mo didn't like Penguin's answer either.

"Maybe he sells things on Ebay," said Hippo, thoughtfully.

Mo didn't mind that answer as much but he knew it wasn't right.

"You're all wrong," said Mo. "Uncle Dink is a computer software engineer. What I want to know is what does a software engineer do all day long if he doesn't go to an office?"

Monkey said, "Go and ask his wife!"

Mo said, "Uncle Dink isn't married. He lives alone somewhere."

"Then he just sleeps all day, like a log." Hippo thought that would be the best thing to do if you lived on your own.

"Can you make easy money by sleeping all day?" Monkey asked. Then he exclaimed, "I know! Uncle Dink must be a frog."

"What do you mean, a frog? Don't be so rude about my uncle," said Mo.

Mo couldn't allow anyone to be rude about Uncle Dink.

But Monkey said:

"I don't mean a frog that sits in a bog,
A frog that's green and slimy.
I mean a dude who stares at a screen
Till his eyes 'bulge out and he's never seen.

A google-eyed geek, a computer freak!"

"Don't be stupid, Monkey!" Penguin said. "You're always so full of rubbish. Why don't we all go to Mo's uncle's flat and have a look. Then we can find out what he does all day long."

The boys set off and soon arrived at the apartment block where Uncle Dink was staying.

"Freeze!"

Hardly had they get through glass sliding door when a security guard shouted at them.

"This is not a place where kids can play!" he yelled.

Monkey cheekily replied, "Do we look like we're here to play my man?"

The security guard stared at them carefully. These boys were dressed well and looked serious. They didn't look like they were going to muck about.

"Then what are you doing here?" he asked.

"We're looking for someone," said Mo.

"Who? Which floor and which flat? What's the number?"

The only thing Mo knew was that Uncle Dink lived on the twenty-ninth floor.

"There are so many people on the twenty-ninth floor. How do I know which one you are looking for?" replied the guard.

Mo said, "My Uncle Dink is a brand new human and he has brightly coloured hair."

"Oh, HIM! He's just gone out," grinned the guard.

"Has he gone to work?" asked Mo.

"Maybe he has, maybe he hasn't," said the guard. "He goes out about mid-day and comes back *very*

late. He doesn't wear a suit or a tie so I haven't a clue what he does every day."

The people who lived in this apartment block were all business people. Their companies rented them flats when they had to come to the city to work. The men wore suits, the women wore high heels. That's why Uncle Dink looked so different and the guard knew who the boys were looking for.

But even the security guard didn't know what Uncle Dink did everyday.

It was a mystery.

DOUBLE SHOT LATTE
WITH A DASH OF
VANILLA

Now Mo's friends were *really* curious and they too became fascinated by Uncle Dink even though they had never met him. He was a mystery, and there was nothing they liked more than a good mystery.

Uncle Dink earned a lot of money but he didn't go out to work. What exactly *did* he do?

The winter holidays were coming and the boys had

already broken up from school. What were they going to do?

Monkey said, "Mo, Uncle Dink goes out at mid-day every day, doesn't he? So let's follow him and see where he goes."

Mo's Uncle Dink had now become THEIR uncle. They all called him Uncle Dink!

Monkey's plans were usually ridiculous, but this was a good one. They dashed to the apartment block. It was eleven o'clock sharp – well before mid-day.

Mo noticed a bookshop opposite the building. They decided to go in there and pretend to be choosing books, then they could watch the apartment building.

But the bookshop owner had a different idea.

"Out! Out!" shouted the man, as if he was shooing away a flock of geese. "There are no Chinese books here. We only sell books in English."

"How ridiculous," argued Monkey. "Do you sell books to Chinese people or English people?"

Monkey always found a chance to argue with somebody.

"Boys, don't make trouble here," the book-shop owner scolded. "These books are for people who can read English. Can *you* read English?"

"How would you know whether we could or not," replied Monkey.

Each of them picked up an English book and pretended to read.

"You kids… ow, ow, ouch…"

The bookshop owner always got toothache when he got angry. He went as white as a sheet, put his hand to his mouth and could not utter another word. Suddenly—

"He's out!" Mo yelled.

They shut their books at once and stared at the man walking through the glass door. He was dressed all in black, wearing a baggy cotton jacket with a hood and baggy trousers with metal zip and studs, shining in the winter sun.

"Mo, you said Uncle Dink's hair was rainbow-coloured, but…"

Mo saw that Uncle Dink's hair had changed to black. There were only some wisps of silver curly hair at the front.

"Mo, is that really Uncle Dink?" asked Hippo.

"Definitely. I know my own uncle!" Mo was the first to dash out. "Come on. Let's follow him!"

"But, his hair…"

Hippo was not very imaginative, but Monkey was.

"He's had his hair dyed. He can have it dyed any way he likes. He's a brand new human."

Uncle Dink had long legs and they had to hurry to keep up with him. They had planned to shadow him like special agents on TV – sometimes hiding behind trees

or sometimes standing in front of a shop window but secretly looking sideways at the person they followed. But Uncle Dink walked so fast, they couldn't do either of those things.

Uncle Dink walked into a café and sat at a table by the window, where a beam of warm sunlight fell on him. He took off his black cotton jacket and revealed a sloppy white sweatshirt with grey leather patches on the shoulders and elbows.

"Let's guess what Uncle Dink will do when he's finished his coffee," said Mo.

Nobody had a clue. They decided to continue following him after he'd finished his coffee and find out.

They heard Uncle Dink ordering "a double shot latte with a dash of vanilla". The coffee was served and Uncle Dink sipped a little. Then he took out a laptop from his bag. He put it on the table then took out a pile papers from the bag and put them beside the laptop.

"What is Uncle Dink doing?"

"He seems to be working,"

"Why does he work in the café?"

They decided they would have to go and ask him.

Mo was the first to enter the café. He went straight to Uncle Dink.

"Uncle Dink!"

Uncle Dink raised his head and looked at Mo, Penguin, Hippo and Monkey, as if he had known them for a long time. Then he pointed at the chairs and said, casually, "Pull up some chairs, boys. What can I do for you?"

The boys asked Uncle Dink whether he was working here.

"Yes."

Uncle Dink would not say another word.

"Why are you working here and not in an office?"

"It's cozy."

Two words this time.

They boys didn't know what else to say. They tried to feel the coziness. The café was quiet, the sunlight was gentle, sentimental songs played on the CD player. The table was clean, the flower on the table was blossoming, and the air in the room smelled good...

It *was* cozy – really cozy!

Uncle Dink looked very busy. He kept looking at the screen and then at his papers, as if Mo and his friends were not there at all.

It was nearly lunchtime. Mo was getting hungry and his tummy was rumbling.

Mo asked, "Uncle Dink, what are we going to eat for lunch?"

Uncle Dink crooked his finger and a waiter with black bow tie came to him. "Sandwiches. Five."

Five sandwiches were served in no time. Penguin and his friends thought sandwiches were snacks and not proper meals. But Uncle Dink ate up his sandwich and went on with his work, as if they were not there at all.

Penguin said, "Uncle Dink, you haven't had your lunch yet."

Uncle Dink answered without looking up, "The sandwich was my lunch."

From his manner, they knew Uncle Dink was getting a bit fed up with them and they didn't think they'd get any more food out of him.

They left the café and decided that they now knew the kind of person a brand new human was.

Monkey said, "A brand new human works in a café and drinks double shot latte with a dash of vanilla."

Penguin said, "A brand new human eats a sandwich for lunch."

Hippo said, "A brand new human has patches on his sweat top."

Mo said, "A brand new human changes the colour of his hair frequently. You will never know what his hair will look like from day to day."

They all agreed that Uncle Dink, brand new human, was one cool human being!

BRAND NEW FOOD

Uncle Dink worked in the café on weekdays, but what did he do at weekends? This was a question that interested both Mo and his friends.

Mo called his uncle. "Uncle Dink, can I come and see you at the weekend, please?"

"OK!" said Uncle Dink, as talkative as ever. He would not waste an extra word.

"And can I bring my friends? You've met them before, the other day in the café, and you bought them sandwiches."

"OK."

Uncle Dink's voice sounded sleepy, and Mo could hear the sound of keys being tapped. Uncle Dink must be using a hands-free phone so he could work on his laptop at the same time.

"Yeah!" Mo yelled in joy. He hadn't thought Uncle Dink would want to see him and his friends on a weekend.

Mo called Penguin, "Penguin, Uncle Dink's invited us round to his flat."

Mo called Monkey, "Monkey, Uncle Dink's invited us to visit him."

"Really?" Monkey screamed on the other side of the line. "Visiting a brand new human at the weekend, I wonder what it will be like?"

"A brand new weekend," Mo answered.

Monkey sounded a bit worried. "Mo, will we become brand new boys after visiting a brand new human at the weekend?"

Let him worry. Mo didn't care.

Mo called Hippo. "Hippo, Uncle Dink invited us to his flat at the weekend."

At once Hippo became very nervous. "What…what kind of clothes should I wear? Should I have my hair…dyed too?"

Mo almost laughed his head off. Hippo often had weird ideas.

It was Saturday morning, around mid-day. The boys went to the apartment block and up to the twenty-ninth floor. They pressed the doorbell. Uncle Dink came to the door. There was a smell of coffee and toast in the flat.

Penguin's stomach began to rumble.

Penguin asked Mo in a loud voice if he was hungry.

"OK, boys, I can take a hint. Let's all go out for something to eat," said Uncle Dink, laughing.

"Uncle Dink, will we be eating sandwiches again?" asked Penguin.

Penguin wanted more than a sandwich for his lunch.

"Sandwiches are my working lunches. Today is Saturday, not a working day, so don't worry, we will eat a proper lunch," said Uncle Dink.

Uncle Dink said that if he ate more than a sandwich on a working day, he would feel too sleepy to work in the afternoon.

"Did you hear that, Penguin?" Monkey said. "No

wonder you're always so dozy at school in the afternoon – you eat too much!"

Penguin's stomach rumbled again. Now he was too hungry to argue with Monkey. The only thing that worried him was what he was going to eat for his lunch.

"OK guys," said Uncle Dink. "Give your parents a ring and let them know that Mo's Uncle Dink is taking you out for lunch."

They walked for ages before they came to a little house with green tiles and white walls. It didn't look anything like a restaurant. Penguin was worried... all that walking had made him even hungrier.

"This is it, guys," said Uncle Dink. "You won't have eaten anywhere like this before, I bet!"

Uncle Dink walked into the little house and they all sat down on wooden benches in front of a long wooden table. A man with a ponytail and an earring in one ear came to serve them. Uncle Dink said that this was the boss of the restaurant but he was also a poet.

No sooner had they sat down than the poet handed them two menus – one for cold dishes and one for hot.

Uncle Dink said the boys could each choose one dish.

Mo opened the cold dish menu. What he saw were not names of food dishes he recognised, but weird things like:

Standing by a tree stump waiting for a rabbit to come

and

Where fishes swim in waters deep

and

How many wings to fly to the moon?

Who could work out what meals these strange sentences stood for?

Mo hadn't got a clue so he decided to order something called *Not Tomato in a Pickle*. Mo didn't like tomatoes, so as long as the food was *not* tomato he knew he'd be OK. He couldn't wait to find out what it really was.

Penguin ordered something called *A Bad Hair Day.*
Then it was Monkey's turn.

"What do you suppose is a *Standing Fish*? I'm going
to order that."

When it was Hippo's turn, he
ordered something he thought
sounded really adventurous.

"I'm going to have *Dragon
Tongues with Snow and Ice.*"

"Well, you're all really
smart," said Uncle Dink. "Now
we have a cold dish, two hot
dishes and a soup."

The waitress wrote down
the names of dishes and repeated them as if she was
singing. "Your cold dish is *Not Tomato in a Pickle.*
Your hot dishes are *Dragon Tongues with Snow and
Ice*, and *A Standing Fish*. The soup is *A Bad Hair Day.*"

While they were waiting for their food, Mo looked
at the other people in the restaurant – they all looked
like brand new humans to him.

The cold dish came – *Not Tomato in a Pickle*. Mo
was worried, it looked just like a plate of small
tomatoes, cut up.

Mo, Penguin, Monkey and Hippo picked up their chopsticks and put a little *Not Tomato in a Pickle* in their mouths.

"Ha Ha," said Mo, relieved. "It's pickled radish."

But these were not normal radishes, they were small radishes like red dates with red skin and a tender taste. They were *delicious*!

The first hot dish to arrive was *A Standing Fish*. Fish was usually served flat on the plate, but this fish was standing up, with one eye glaring at Penguin and the other eye glaring at Monkey. The boys were too scared to pick up their chopsticks in case the fish bit them! But the waitress came and lay the fish flat on the plate, then cut it into little pieces for everyone to have some.

The next hot dish was Hippo's choice: *Dragon Tongues on Snow and ice*. The boys were amazed because this dish wasn't just hot – it was SIZZLING, just like dragons' tongues! When the sizzling died down, the boys could see it was strips of crispy beef with hot chilli peppers. There were side dishes of plain cold yoghourt and coconut flakes, for the snow and ice. Everyone loved Hippo's choice.

The last one was the soup, *A Bad Hair Day*. When they saw it, Mo and his friends fell about laughing – it was just a bowl of birds' nest soup!

What a special meal this was, it was something really different. Trust Uncle Dink to come here. This brand new human really was different from normal humans!

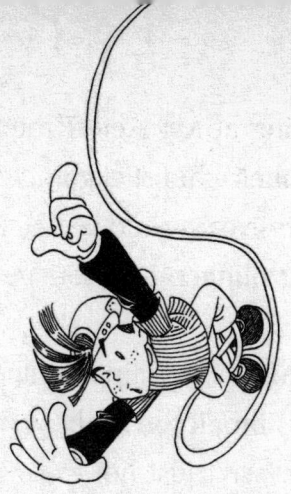

THE BUNGEE JUMP

After they'd finished their meal, Uncle Dink asked the boys what they wanted to do for the rest of the day. The boys didn't really care what they did, as long as they could do it with this brand new human.

"OK," said Uncle Dink. "Let's do something *challenging*. How about bungee jumping?"

The boys all gasped.

Hippo said "yes" without hesitation.

Mo also said he was up for it.

Monkey, unlike Hippo and Mo, wouldn't say "yes" or "no" until he had thought about it carefully.

"Do we need to jump off a cliff?" he asked.

"Don't be stupid," said Penguin. "Nobody can jump off a cliff and live."

"But that's what bungee jumping is, isn't it?" said Monkey.

Uncle Dink said, "That's right. But it's quite safe. You have a harness on all the time. My friend Canary is the jump master."

"*Canary*," the boys all said at once. "What kind of a name is that?"

"Oh, you'll understand when you see him!" said Uncle Dink, mysteriously. "Now, are you up for a bit of bungee jumping?"

"OK," Monkey said. "I'll do it. Penguin, what about you?"

Penguin said it would depend on how strong the harness was.

Uncle Dink and the boys got into a taxi which took them out of the city. It wound around twisty roads and up a mountain side.

Halfway up the mountain the taxi stopped. Uncle Dink point up towards the top of the mountain.

"Have you seen that before? That's Hawk Beak Cliff. That's where we're jumping from."

Penguin went deathly pale.

Monkey's voice trembled. "But it's so high. And what's down there?"

Uncle Dink smiled. "An abyss," he whispered.

Everyone knew that an abyss was a bottomless place.

Monkey went very quiet.

"Do you know the origin of bungee jumping?" asked Uncle Dink.

The boys didn't so Uncle Dink explained.

"Bungee jumping originated in Vanuatu, an island country in the south pacific. It is a ceremony there, when a boy becomes a man. It's a test for a boy's strength, will, faith and intelligence."

Monkey asked, "What if you're too scared to jump?"

"Then you don't become a man," whispered Hippo.

Hippo was excited; he was very sporty. He couldn't wait to jump.

Penguin wasn't excited – he was scared. Penguin was a bit of a baby.

Monkey had a think and asked Uncle Dink, "What will I become if I don't jump?"

Uncle Dink laughed, "You'll stay the same, don't worry. Nobody HAS to jump if they don't want to."

But nobody wanted to say they didn't want to – if one jumped, they all would.

BECOMING MEN

The taxi arrived at the top of Hawk Beak Cliff. Mo opened the left door and Hippo opened the right – both were longing to get out. Monkey, however, pretended to have tummy ache. And Penguin pretended he was sleeping.

"OW," Monkey cried, clutching his stomach. "I think the Standing Fish must have been really bad."

"Impossible!" said Uncle Dink. "We all ate it, so we'd all have tummy ache if it had been bad."

"He's pretending!" said Mo. He got back in the taxi

and tickled him. Monkey was very ticklish and he started yelling:

"Ha-ha, spare me my life!"

"Well, stop pretending, then," said Mo, sternly.

Now only Penguin was left in the taxi, pretending to be asleep.

"Wake up, Penguin, wake up."

Penguin replied with a snore.

"Oh well," said Uncle Dink. "All the more chocolate for us."

Penguin immediately woke up and got out of the taxi.

The four boys stood on top of Hawk Beak Cliff. They looked up and there were blue sky and white clouds. They looked down and saw... just a dark, bottomless valley below. Then they noticed there were other people there, some with harnesses already on,

others looking excited and happy, just taking their harnesses off.

Then Mo saw a man with bright yellow hair, and "Jump Master" written on his jacket – that must be Uncle Dink's friend, Canary. Mo was pleased – Canary looked like another brand new human.

"Yo, Canary," said Uncle Dink, "Meet my very special nephew, Mo, and his very special friends."

"Hi, little fellows, are you ready to jump?" said Canary.

"Mo, are you scared?" Uncle Dink asked, trying to catch his nephew out.

"No, I'm not afraid, not at all."

But he was.

"I'll jump first, then it's your turn," said Uncle Dink.

Canary helped Uncle Dink put on his harness. He stood at the edge of the cliff, with his eyes closed a little. He took a deep breath and shot out.

Uncle Dink stretched out his arms and legs and dived into the deep valley. He looked like a flying hawk with great, wide wings.

"See? It's like flying," said Canary. "It gives you a wonderful feeling. Which one of you is going first?"

Mo looked at Hippo.

Hippo looked at Mo.

Mo asked Canary, "Will we turn from boys to men after we jump?"

"Most definitely," said Canary. He seemed serious. "Courage is very important for a man. So... Take courage, young man and get the harness on."

Hippo was helped into the harness. He stood like a puppet before its strings are pulled, motionless at the cliff edge not daring to open his eyes to look around or down.

When they saw Hippo hesitating, Monkey and Penguin started chanting.

"Hippo, jump, jump!"

"Hippo, you'll be a man if you jump!"

Hippo threw himself out and hurtled down into the abyss... then bounced back up again.

"Now Mo, it's your turn," said the others.

Monkey and Penguin gripped Mo's arms, in case he tried to run away.

"Let me go!" he yelled.

Mo fought them off and let Canary help him with the harness. He approached the cliff, solemn and determined. He was *really* scared – if the harness failed, he would surely die. He looked down.

Aaaargh! he thought. The ground was kilometres away!

Monkey and Penguin made an awful fuss behind him.

"Mo, Uncle Dink has jumped, and Hippo has jumped, why won't you jump too?"

"Mo, just jump. It'll be great. You'll feel like a pet bird that's been let out of its cage."

Penguin and Monkey sniggered.

Mo didn't jump. He stared at a cloud in the sky, which was travelling freely. How Mo wished that he was the cloud, without any sense of fear.

Mo was too scared to jump and he felt ashamed. How could he become a man if he was too afraid to jump.

No, Mo had to be a man—

He leaped.

His ears filled with a rush of wind. His body felt so light that it flew freely between sky and earth, like a bird.

Mo's fear had flown away with this flight. Now he was a bird. He was enjoying the freedom and happiness of being a bird.

Hippo had jumped, and Mo had jumped too.

But Monkey and Penguin still couldn't pluck up courage.

When Mo and Hippo had bounced back up to the cliff, they felt good. They felt they were real men.

"Penguin and Monkey, don't you want to be brave men?"

Hippo and Mo were goading them. Penguin's face was really pasty and Monkey's spindly legs kept trembling.

"Go and jump!" Hippo said to Penguin. "You'll feel so light when you're in the sky."

Then Mo said, "You'll feel like a little bird after you jump."

"Yes," said Uncle Dink. "There's nothing quite like a bungee jump to make you feel on top of the world!"

"Really?" Monkey was persuaded.

Monkey jumped.

When he came back up again, he was laughing.

"Jump, Penguin," he whispered. "You can't fall to the ground with the harness round your waist."

Penguin just didn't want to go, he wanted to cry. But he knew he couldn't cry in front of his friends and he certainly couldn't cry in front of the brand new human, Uncle Dink. He had to jump. If he didn't jump, he would remain a timid boy while his friends would be courageous men. They might no longer want to be his friend.

Penguin shot out.

A success for everybody!

"May I declare," said Uncle Dink, "that from now on, Mo, Hippo, Monkey and Penguin are not boys any more – they are men!"

WHEN IS A PARENT NOT A PARENT?

The parents' evening was to be held straight after the winter holidays. Mo's parents were away on a business trip and couldn't attend the meeting. So Mo told Ms Qin that he would be representing himself.

"No way!" Ms Qin said. "One of your parents must come."

But if they were away, how could they go? Mo wondered.

Then Mo had an idea!

Uncle Dink was living in Mo's flat while Mo's parents were away. He was supposed to be taking care of Mo, though actually Mo was taking care of himself.

"Uncle Dink, will you please attend the parents' evening for me tomorrow?"

Uncle Dink knew that Mo was mischievous at school and didn't really want to represent such a naughty boy.

"Can I say no?"

"Of course not. Ms Qin told me that any other parents could be absent but not *my* parents."

Mo knew how strict Ms Qin was and he didn't want to disobey her.

But Uncle Dink was worried that he might get the blame for having a mischievous nephew.

Mo knew that his father, Mr Ma, had been blamed for Mo's behaviour every time he'd attended a parents' meeting. But Mo didn't dare tell his uncle this.

Mo decided to change the subject. "Uncle Dink, if you dress like that, Ms Qin will not like it. She's quite old."

Uncle Dink was wearing his black leather jeans and jacket, the one with zips and studs. He'd also dyed his hair again, this time it was red and green.

So, in order to make Ms Qin happy, Uncle Dink dyed his hair black again, and put on one of Mr Ma's black business suits and a tie. He looked funny in this suit because he was much taller than Mr Ma, and the trouser legs were too short for him.

Mo didn't think it would be safe to let Uncle Dink go to the parents meeting alone, so he went along with him. On their way to school, Mo kept on badgering Uncle Dink.

"Uncle Dink, Ms Qin might ask you to stay and have a quiet word with her after the meeting. You have to listen to whatever she says. Be patient and keep nodding your head... and one more thing, remember to smile all the time, that's very important."

"I don't like smiling," grumbled Uncle Dink.

Uncle Dink was telling the truth. Brand new humans seldom smiled. They were too cool for that.

"But you must smile. Otherwise, Ms Qin will think that you do not respect her."

The parents' evening turned out to be a real nightmare for Uncle Dink. He just couldn't understand why Mo's teacher had so much to say.

Finally the meeting came to an end. But the last thing Ms Qin said was, "Mo's parent, please stay."

The other parents were weird. They didn't seem at all tired after such a long evening. They all wanted to ask Ms Qin questions and Uncle Dink thought he would be there for ever. He did notice, though, that Ms Qin seemed very friendly to these parents.

He waited for ages until all the other parents were gone. Ms Qin began to notice Uncle Dink, sitting alone in the empty classroom looking like an obedient pupil.

"You're..."

"I'm Mo's parent... just for this evening."

Uncle Dink stood up respectfully. He wanted to smile at Ms Qin but failed. He only managed a slight curl of his top lip.

Ms Qin looked at Uncle Dink, from his head to his feet, and vice versa. She paid particular attention to his suit, the sleeves of which barely came past his elbows, and the trousers to his knees.

She suspected him of stealing it.

"I'm Mo's uncle," said Uncle Dink.

"Why couldn't Mo's father come?"

"He's away on a business trip."

"What about his mother?"

"She's with him."

Ms Qin stared at Uncle Dink. Her gaze, sharp as a dagger, could penetrate any disguise.

"Do you have permission to represent Mo's parents?"

"I'm afraid so."

"What do you mean by that?"

"Er... nothing," said Uncle Dink.

"OK, now let's talk about Mo."

Ms Qin began her lengthy speech.

Uncle Dink was miles away. He didn't know what Ms Qin was talking about, but he did remember what Mo had told him. He just kept nodding and smiling and didn't say a word.

Being a brand new human, nodding was much easier for Uncle Dink than smiling. So he kept on nodding like a hen picking up grains from the earth. He tried to smile but could not. The muscles of his face went into spasm.

"What, what...what's wrong with you?" cried Ms Qin.

Ms Qin stopped talking about Mo. She was worried that Uncle Dink was suffering.

"Are you sick?" she asked him.

Ms Qin thought Uncle Dink was having a fit. She backed toward the classroom door, step by step, turned around and shouted, "Stay there, I'll get some help."

"Ha-ha! Ha-ha!" Uncle Dink laughed.

He'd scared Ms Qin off!

KNOWING MO

Uncle Dink wandered out of the classroom and into the playground, where Mo was waiting.

"Uncle Dink!"

Mo ran to his uncle. "Did Ms Qin ask you stay after the other parents left?"

"Yes."

"What did Ms Qin say?"

"She said your schoolwork is terrible and that you are a mischievous pupil," said Uncle Dink.

Things seemed to be getting serious.

Mo was worried. "What did Ms Qin say, exactly?"

Actually, Uncle Dink had no idea what Ms Qin had said. When she gave her lengthy speech, Uncle Dink hadn't really bothered to listen. But since he had gone to the meeting on behalf of Mo's parents, he had to be responsible for him.

"Mo, you have disappointed me," he said, seriously.

Mo felt ashamed. He liked Uncle Dink and he knew Uncle Dink liked him too. He was afraid that Uncle Dink wouldn't like him any more.

"Uncle Dink, I'm not so terrible. You don't know me properly."

There was a small sideways movement of Uncle Dink's lips.

"I mean, you shouldn't just listen to Ms Qin," said Mo. "You ought to listen to other teachers too. For example, Ms Lin."

"Who is Ms Lin?"

"Ms Lin is our drawing teacher," Mo said. Then he leaned forwards and whispered in Uncle Dink's ear, "She is the most beautiful woman in the world."

Mo was sure that if Uncle Dink went to Ms Lin, Ms Lin would definitely say something nice about Mo and then Uncle Dink would like him again.

And now Uncle Dink wanted to see Ms Lin too, not because he wanted to know about Mo but because Mo said she was the most beautiful woman in the world...

"Where is Ms Lin?" Uncle Dink said, "I'll go and see her."

Mo stopped his uncle. "Ms Lin shares an office with Ms Qin."

Uncle Dink didn't want to see Ms Qin again.

"Then what shall we do?" he asked.

Mo had an idea.

"Let's go to the school secretary and ask her to call Ms Lin."

Mo took his uncle to the school office.

"Mrs Han, could you please phone Ms Lin and say there's someone waiting to see her?"

Mrs Han was very short-sighted. She wore a pair of glasses with really thick lenses.

"Who's waiting for Ms Lin?"

Mo pointed at Uncle Dink. "It's him."

Mrs Han approached Uncle Dink and examined him from head to feet, and then from feet to head again. She noticed that Uncle Dink's suit hardly covered his elbows and knees. She thought this suit

was very suspicious.

Mo pulled Mrs Han to the telephone. "Please call Ms Lin quickly. He has something really urgent to speak to her about."

Hearing it was urgent, Mrs Han forgot her suspicion and picked up the telephone, "Ms Lin, there is a man waiting for you in the office. It's urgent."

Someone was running across the playground to the office. She was in a thin red wool sweater, and had no coat on. The winter wind blew her long black hair, and her cheeks were flushed.

"What do you think?" Mo asked proudly, "Isn't she beautiful?"

Uncle Dink hardly had time to answer before Ms Lin was in front of them.

"Who's expecting me? Is it you, Mo?" she said.

Ms Lin was breathless from running.

Mo pointed at his uncle, "It's him."

"You're…"

Ms Lin looked at Uncle Dink and almost laughed out loud seeing his funny suit.

"I'm Mo's uncle," he said. "It's nice to meet you."

"Oh!" Ms Lin said, surprised. "What I can do for you?"

Mo smiled at Ms Lin and said. "Uncle wants to know what I am like at school."

Ms Lin smiled. "Then you should have gone to Ms Qin."

"I've talked to Ms Qin, and Mo said I must speak to you too." Uncle Dink pretended to be a responsible parent. "In your opinion, Ms Lin, what kind of a boy is Mo?"

"Mo is a special boy with many good qualities. And I like him very much… *achoo*!"

Ms Lin sneezed. She was standing in the cold wind with a thin sweater. Uncle Dink said she should go back inside, quickly.

Mo was a little disappointed but at least he now knew that Ms Lin liked him, and that made him feel good about himself.

MATCH-MAKING

Uncle Dink was in his thirties but he wasn't married. Mo's grandparents were very worried about this and they started quizzing Mo about it.

"Mo, your uncle is over thirty. Why doesn't he get married?"

"Brand new humans like him do not marry," replied Mo, wisely.

"But even brand new humans are still humans," Grandpa said. "And humans should get married and have children."

Grandpa and Grandma never disagreed with each

other when talking to people. "That's right. Your uncle's best friend is married with a son old enough for Nursery," said Grandma. "But your uncle doesn't even have a girlfriend to mend his socks."

Mo said, "Well, brand new humans wear socks with air holes in them. They let the air move around their feet."

"And your uncle loses his shoe laces and has to use sticky tape," said Grandpa.

"Brand new humans don't use shoe laces, they use magic tape instead," replied Mo, quickly.

Everything was getting very silly.

Grandpa said, "Well, a man should get married when he's grown up."

Mo thought Grandma and Grandpa were SO old-fashioned. "When I grow up, I will never get married," he declared.

"Nonsense!" Grandpa was getting cross and knocked the table with his palm.

"Don't believe a word he says, he's only a child," laughed Grandma.

"Mo, getting married can bring you good things."

Mo asked, "What kind of good things?"

Grandma was smiling, "Well, when your uncle gets

married, you will have another aunt. And later, you will have another cousin who will be like a little brother or sister to you."

Mo thought, if he had one more aunt, he would get one more present for his birthday. Well, that wouldn't be bad. He continued to think. If he had another cousin, he could play with him or her. When the cousin grew up a bit he could boss him or her around. Well, that wouldn't be bad either. And if the cousin was as naughty as the cousin he already had, Daisy, they could have loads of fun!

So Uncle Dink's marriage would be good for Mo. He agreed with Grandma and Grandpa – Uncle Dink would have to get married.

What kind of girl should Uncle Dink marry?

Grandma said, "She must be a pretty girl."

Grandpa said, "She must be a quiet girl."

Grandma said, "She must be a nice girl."

Grandpa said, "She must be a caring girl."

"Stop it!" Mo shouted, "Do you want Uncle Dink to marry four girls?"

"Mo, what are you talking about?" this time Grandma got angry.

"Yes, four girls." Mo counted with his fingers. "A

pretty girl, a quiet girl, a nice girl and a caring girl. Four girls altogether."

Grandpa and Grandma found their mischievous grandson funny... and annoying.

"We hope your uncle will marry *one* girl who is pretty, quiet, nice and caring."

Mo had an idea!

He knew just the girl for his uncle. He decided that this girl must be Ms Lin and he told his grandparents so.

"Who is Ms Lin?" they said.

"She's the girl you are looking for." Mo got excited.

"Uncle Dink should marry Ms Lin!"

The thought of having Ms Lin as his aunt made Mo want to rush home.

"I must go and see Uncle Dink right now," he said.

"Mo, we will depend on you for our son to be married to Ms Lin!" yelled Grandpa and Grandma.

62

Mo went back home but Uncle Dink was not there. He was still supposed to be looking after Mo while his parents were away, but apart from going to the parents' evening, he hadn't done much else.

Mo decided that since Uncle Dink wasn't in, he could give Ms Lin a call.

"Hello, Ms Lin, do you remember my uncle?" asked Mo when she answered the phone.

Of course she remembered the man in the suspicious suit. Ms Lin laughed.

"Ms Lin, the other day, my uncle didn't have time to listen to you any more because he was worried you might catch a cold in the playground. But he still wants to know more about me at school, and he would like to see you again."

Ms Lin said, "Ms Qin is your class teacher. She can tell your uncle all about your schoolwork."

"But Ms Qin pays more attention to my mischief than to my schoolwork! So you are the better choice."

Ms Lin laughed again. Mo could imagine her smile though he couldn't see it.

Ms Lin couldn't resist such a cheeky boy, so she agreed to see Uncle Dink again.

THE MEETING

Mo had only just put down the phone when Uncle Dink came back.

"Uncle Dink, it's Saturday tomorrow. Are you going to work?"

Uncle Dink took off his shoes and put on his flip flops. "Nope, no work at the weekend."

Mo said, "Then you've got to see Ms Lin."

Uncle Dink couldn't remember who Ms Lin was. "Who's Ms Lin?" he said. "Not another of your teachers who wants to tell me how mischievous you are?"

"You MUST remember her. She is the most beautiful woman in the world," screeched Mo.

"The most beautiful woman in the world?" said Uncle Dink. "I should be so lucky!"

"You met her the other day after the parents' meeting…"

"Oh, her. The teacher who sneezed!"

Mo couldn't believe that his uncle was not excited by the thought of meeting up with Ms Lin again. "Don't you think she is the most beautiful woman in the whole world?"

Uncle Dink didn't want to upset Mo by saying he hadn't found Ms Lin to be especially beautiful. He just said he hadn't really seen her very clearly that day.

"Now you are my fake parent, you have to be responsible for me," continued Mo.

Uncle Dink laughed. "I think you mean 'acting parent', not 'fake parent'."

Mo looked at him. "I know what I mean."

Uncle Dink laughed again. "Mo, what must I do to take my responsibility seriously?"

"You must find out about me from my teacher," said Mo.

"Well, I have talked to your class teacher, Ms Qin, about you," said Uncle Dink "She said your schoolwork was terrible."

"But she's only *one* teacher. You haven't talked to Ms Lin." Mo paused. "Ms Lin is coming here tomorrow."

Uncle Dink collapsed on the sofa. "I don't believe it! It seems I have to spend my valuable weekend on your affairs."

Mo replied, sharply, "It isn't easy being a parent."

The next morning, Mo and Uncle Dink were woken up the doorbell ringing.

"Who can that be? It's so early!" thought Mo.

Mo turned over and fell asleep again.

"Mo, go and open the door," shouted Uncle Dink from his room.

Mo shouted back, "I can't. I'm in my PJs."

Uncle Dink yelled, "Well, I'm in *my* PJs so I can't go either."

Suddenly Mo jumped out of bed. "It must be Ms Lin."

Mo quickly put on a sweater and trousers over his PJs and ran barefoot to the door.

It really was Ms Lin.

"You've only just woken up? Do you know what time it is?" Ms Lin showed him her watch. "Didn't you tell me to come at ten o'clock?" she said.

Mo blushed.

To divert Ms Lin's attention away from himself, he shouted loudly, "Uncle Dink, Ms Lin is here."

Out came Uncle Dink. His hair was multi-coloured. His baggy grey sweat top had big leather patches on the shoulders and elbows. There were a zillion pockets and zippers on his cotton tracksuit trousers.

"Ms Lin, this is my Uncle Dink," said Mo.

Today's Dink was completely different from the one in the suspicious suit that Ms Lin had seen the other day in school.

Ms Lin gave Uncle Dink a shy smile.

Uncle Dink gave an equally shy smile, or rather he twisted his mouth a little.

The two adults were nervous, but Mo was not. He began introduce his uncle to Ms Lin properly. "He's a software engineer, with an annual salary of one hundred thousand Yuan, bonus not included. He is 1.78 metres tall. He likes drinking double-shot latte with a dash of vanilla. He enjoys bungee jumping and eating *A Standing Fish*. He goes to work in a café everyday. He's thirty years old and still single..."

"MO!"

Ms Lin and Uncle Dink stopped Mo at the very same time.

Ms Lin exchanged an embarrassed look with Uncle Dink and said, "Let's talk about Mo."

Uncle Dink nodded. "That's right, let's talk about Mo."

"Let me think…" said Ms Lin, "Mo is like… a child."

Uncle Dink twisted his lips. "Mo *is* a child."

"But what I mean is," continued Ms Lin, "many children are not like children these days. They pretend to be so grown-up. They wear grown-up clothes, they speak in grown-up language, they want to be just like their parents."

Uncle Dink nodded again. "Ms Lin, if my memory serves me right, you told me you *liked* Mo the other day in the school."

"Yes, I do like Mo."

"But from what I remember, teachers only like children who are good at school. Why do you like Mo when he isn't very good at school?"

"Mo is curious, and mischievous. He's a real child. Children learn by making mistakes and then NOT making the same mistakes again. They learn when they can be cheeky, and when they can not be cheeky."

Uncle Dink's eyes sparkled when he listened – he already liked Ms Lin!

NOT GROWING UP

Mo found that Uncle Dink and Ms Lin had something in common – they both liked Mo, and for the same reason – he was mischievous, but he was honest, and kind.

"Mo's drawings are very special," said Ms Lin. "He sees everything from a child's point of view. He breaks the rules and uses bright, bold colours. I don't think Mo draws perfectly, but he draws with humour and imagination. I hope his parents and you know how talented he is."

Having said everything she could about Mo, Ms Lin stood up to go.

"Ms Lin, please don't leave," said Mo. He stared fixedly at Uncle Dink.

Ms Lin asked, "Are there any other questions?"

"We've talked enough about Mo, but I still have some more questions." Uncle Dink looked around, "But I'd rather go somewhere else, somewhere less formal than Mo's flat. Ms Lin, do you like bars?"

"What sort of bars?"

"Well, a pub, Internet café, juice bar, water bar, snack bar, pottery-making bar, toy bar, ball bar, piano bar...which kind of bar do you like?"

Mo leaped in and said, "I like toy bars."

"Be quiet. I'm not asking you!" said Uncle Dink. "We will go to a bar Ms Lin chooses."

Ms Lin had no alternative but to say she'd prefer a water bar, thinking that drinking a glass of water wouldn't take too much time.

There was almost everything in the so-called water bar.

Ms Lin ordered a glass of mineral water, nothing else.

Uncle Dink ordered a double-shot latte with a dash of vanilla.

Mo ordered lots of things: an ice-cream, some

fruit salad and a slice of Black Forest cake.

Ms Lin sipped the water. "Now Mo's uncle, what did you want to ask me?"

Uncle Dink, enjoying his coffee, completely forgot what he wanted to ask Ms Lin.

"Er, er, what I wanted to ask you was..." Uncle Dink looked at Mo for a hint. "Mo, remind me..."

Mo was busy enjoying his ice-cream and didn't answer. "*Slurp... Slurp...*"

"Oh, I remember!" Uncle Dink clapped his forehead, "Why does a person like me, already thirty, love watching cartoons, reading cartoons and playing e-pets?"

"Ah," said Ms Lin. "You are like Peter Pan. You don't want to grow up."

Uncle Dink burst into laughter. It was the first time Mo had seen this brand new human laughing like that.

"Please don't laugh!" Ms Lin talked to Uncle Dink as if he was a student in her class. "Grown people who don't want to grow up are usually workaholics – they work very hard. Then, when they are away from work, they try hard to relax: watching and reading things that are easy, like cartoons. Playing with things that don't involve too much brain work, like e-pets and hanging about with kids like Mo. These are all good ways to relax."

"You're brilliant, Ms Lin!" Uncle Dink was totally convinced. "When I'm exhausted, I often think, 'how wonderful it would be to be a kid again, a kid like Mo, without worries and pressure, always happy'."

It was the first time Mo had ever heard someone say he wanted to be a kid like him. And the person who had said it was Uncle Dink, the man he adored so much. Since Uncle Dink had come back, Mo had wanted to be just like him. Now Uncle Dink wanted to be like Mo!

Mo's world was becoming more and more confusing.

Ms Lin stood up to go. "Have you finished your questions, Mo's uncle? I've got to go."

"Wait a minute please, Ms Lin," implored Mo.

Mo stopped Ms Lin and made faces at Uncle Dink to drop him a hint.

"Ms Lin, would you like to go somewhere special, somewhere that an Art teacher would like?"

"Where?"

"A Pottery-making bar called The Ceramic Café."

Ms Lin clasped her hands, "Oh yes, I've been meaning to go there for ages!"

Mo also clasped his hands, "Me too!"

"Then we'll go right now." Uncle Dink took out his mobile. "I'll phone Canary. He's got a car so he can drive us there."

Mo didn't want anyone else to come with them. Canary might interfere with his match-making plans for Ms Lin and Uncle Dink.

Mo snatched the mobile from Uncle Dink. "No, let's just the three of us go. We don't want Canary as well."

"We can't get there without Canary. We need a car. The Ceramic Cafe's a long way from here."

Mo had no choice. Canary was going with them whether he liked it or not.

DUCKS CROSSING THE ROAD

Canary arrived in a crazy jeep, as yellow as his hair.

Uncle Dink introduced him to Ms Lin. "This is my friend, Canary."

Ms Lin shook hands with Canary, "Nice to meet you, Canary. I'm one of Mo's teachers."

Ms Lin thought the name "Canary" was really odd, and so was this man's hair. It was bright yellow!

Canary held her hand and would not let it go. "They didn't have such beautiful teachers when I was at school," he said, looking straight into Ms Lin's eyes.

Mo didn't like Canary holding Ms Lin's hand and he didn't like Canary looking into Ms Lin's eyes like that. He walked up to them and separated their hands.

They got into the jeep and Uncle Dink sat in the front seat with Canary. Mo and Ms Lin were in the back.

As soon as they moved off, Canary turned his head and tried to speak to Ms Lin.

"Ms Lin..."

"You mustn't turn round to speak to Ms Lin when you're driving," said Mo. "It's dangerous. But Uncle Dink can."

Canary adjusted the rear-view mirror so he could see Ms Lin clearly.

They drove out of the city and into the suburbs.

Canary didn't turn around to speak with Ms Lin again, but Mo noticed he kept on looking at her in the mirror instead of watching where he was going.

"Look out!" Uncle Dink shouted.

"Ducks! Ducks!" Mo and Ms Lin screamed at the same time.

A family of ducks waddled across the road in a line. It was too late to brake. Canary turned the steering

wheel sharply. The jeep missed the ducks but it struck a traffic sign. The jeep wasn't damaged and no one was hurt. But the traffic sign was completely wrecked.

Canary and Uncle Dink jumped out to look at the ducks.

The ducks were safe and sound, waddling along as if nothing had happened.

Canary made excuses for his bad driving. "Dink, you saw those ducks breaking the traffic rules. It wasn't my fault."

"Do you think ducks know traffic rules? It was your fault for not looking at the road."

There was nobody there. They could just drive away, but there was a problem with the traffic sign.

Uncle Dink talked to Canary for a long time, and then took out his mobile.

Mo and Ms Lin got out of the jeep.

Mo said, "Why don't we just go?"

Uncle Dink answered, "We'll go after we have paid for the damage. As good citizens, we must pay for any damage we have done."

"Who are you going to pay?" Mo looked around. "There's no one here."

"I've called the police. They'll tell us what to do," replied Uncle Dink.

Quite soon, a policeman on a motorbike drew up. "What happened?" he asked taking out his notebook.

"It was a family of ducks…"

"Ducks?" The policeman was confused.

"A family of ducks crossed the road and broke the traffic rules. They are mainly to be blamed. But…" Canary changed the subject, "I shall not argue with ducks. They don't know any better. So, we will pay the cost of the damage to the traffic sign."

The policeman laughed, as did Ms Lin.

The policeman told them to follow him to the nearest police station, where he handed them over to another officer.

The policeman on duty was very serious. His piercing eyes looked at their faces one by one. When he got to Mo, Mo pointed at Canary and said, "It wasn't me. It was him."

Canary said, "It wasn't me either. It was a family of ducks."

Canary told the policeman about the ducks crossing the road and breaking the traffic rules.

"Nonsense!" said the policeman, "Why did the traffic cop bring you here if it's ducks who are the criminals?"

Ms Lin could not watch them being wronged and do nothing.

"I was there and I will vouch for what really happened," she said, persuasively.

"Who are you?" the policeman asked.

"I'm a teacher," replied Ms Lin.

The policeman still thought they were wasting his time.

"It's natural to pay for any damage that's been done. What's the problem?" Uncle Dink did not want to waste time. "Come on, just tell us how much we should pay."

"I'll decide after I have inspected the scene of the accident."

The policeman looked at the two men. He looked at Uncle Dink's stripy hair and at Canary's yellow hair. *What have we here?* he thought. He just could not believe that people who looked like that would voluntarily come to pay for the damage.

ART WORKS

After inspecting the scene of the accident, the policeman said that 780 Yuan should be paid.

Uncle Dink and Canary were brand new humans. They never paid cash for anything they bought, they always used credit cards. The policeman said he could not accept a credit card payment. Uncle Dink and Canary both emptied their pockets, but didn't have enough cash between them to pay the fine. So Ms Lin had to lend them 100 Yuan.

Mo asked, "Are we still going to the pottery-making bar?"

"Of course we are." said Uncle Dink. "If not, why did we come so far?"

"But you haven't got any money!" Mo reminded them.

"It doesn't matter. I'll pay," said Ms Lin.

Ms Lin was beginning to think of Canary and Dink as good friends.

"No way!" said Uncle Dink. "The owner of the pottery-making bar is our friend. He'll let us owe him the money."

The Ceramic Café was in a little house, totally made of logs. The manager, a tall young man with  long hair, looked like an artist. There were several people in the bar and only two potters' wheels were free. Ms Lin and Mo hadn't been there before, so they shared the two potters' wheels with Canary and Uncle Dink.

Mo wanted Uncle Dink and Ms Lin to share a wheel, so he quickly said to Canary, "I want to use a wheel with you."

"Go and learn from your uncle!" said Canary, pushing Mo to Uncle Dink. "I had enough trouble trying to persuade you to do that bungee jump!"

Mo certainly didn't want Ms Lin to know that he had almost been too scared to jump the other day, so he quickly went over and joined Uncle Dink.

Uncle Dink put a block of clay on to the wheel, pressed the board with his foot and the wheel began to go round.

Uncle Dink asked Mo what he wanted to make. Mo answered, "Anything." He was a little absent-minded and kept watching Canary and Ms Lin. He heard Canary boasting, "We will use our hands and our brains to give life to this piece of clay!"

Uncle Dink held Mo's hands and gently put them on the clay.

"Feel it first and we will make a ball," he said.

A ball is the simplest thing to start with on a pottery wheel. Uncle Dink hoped Mo could enjoy feeling the shape form.

But Mo couldn't feel anything. He kept looking at Canary, who was holding Ms Lin's hands, saying "Blah, blah, blah," all the time.

"Uncle Dink, look at Canary!"

"Why are you looking at him?" Uncle Dink would not even raise his head,  "Don't you want to learn how to make pottery?"

Mo was not in the mood for making pottery. He was upset – his match-making was all going wrong. He wanted Uncle Dink and Ms Lin to fall in love. He wanted Uncle Dink and Ms Lin to get married!

Mo walked over to Canary and Ms Lin.

Canary, holding Ms Lin's hands, had produced a cylinder out of the clay on the wheel. It seems that they were making a pot or jar.

"Mo, why are you watching us, instead of learning from your uncle?"

"My uncle isn't a very good teacher. I want to learn from you," pleaded Mo.

"Go away, Mo!" said Canary. "Don't be a pest."

Mo said, "It's you who is being a pest!"

"Mo, come and sit here. We'll change places," said Ms Lin, standing up, "I'll go and learn from your uncle."

Canary watched, helplessly, as Ms Lin went over to Uncle Dink. He didn't want Uncle Dink to hold Ms Lin's hands. *What a pest that Mo is*, he thought.

Mo touched the cylinder on the wheel. This time, he felt the smoothness of the clay, but when he looked over to see how Ms Lin was doing with Uncle Dink, he was disappointed to see that Uncle wasn't holding her hands. He was just standing by her side, showing her what to do, like a teacher and pupil in a class. But Mo didn't want Uncle Dink to be Ms Lin's *teacher*, he wanted him to be her *husband*!

THE NOT-SO-PERFECT BEAUTY

Mo still hadn't persuaded Uncle Dink that Ms Lin was the perfect person for him to marry. But Mo wasn't a boy to give up easily. After a few days, he decided to do a little more prodding.

"Uncle Dink, what do you think of Ms Lin?" he asked.

"Who?" said Uncle Din. "Should I know who you mean?"

"What?" Mo shouted in surprise, "You've only just

met each other! We went to the pottery cafe together, we almost bumped into some ducks, she lent you and Canary some money to pay the fine... you MUST remember her."

"Ah... Ms Lin is too perfect to remember," replied Uncle Din, mysteriously.

It seemed that Uncle Dink didn't really like perfect girls.

Mo thought hard: did he know anyone that wasn't quite so perfect?

Then Mo had an idea. He had once had a home tutor to help him with his English. Her name was Miss Zhang and Mo remembered that she had the most enormous mouth – she was not perfect in his eyes.

Shortly after Miss Zhang became Mo's tutor, she refused to teach him any more because every time she came to teach him, Mo would just stare at her mouth. At first, she thought he did so to watch the correct way of pronouncing English words. She purposely opened her mouth wide and spoke very slowly, to let Mo see more clearly how English was spoken. But when she did this, Mo just wanted to ask her lots of questions like:

"Miss Zhang, when you eat dumplings, do you bite each one once or twice?"

Miss Zhang answered his question, even though it had nothing to do with the English lesson. "Once," she replied.

"Most people bite twice," said Mo, cheekily.

Miss Zhang did not get angry with Mo that time, but when more and more questions came she began to get a little bit peeved.

Mo once found that Miss Zhang's lipstick was smudged.

"Miss Zhang, you haven't put on your very lipstick well," he said.

Miss Zhang was embarrassed and replied crossly, "I know, I had to rush to get here this morning."

"Miss Zhang – can you eat a whole hard boiled egg in one bite, like my friend Hippo?" asked Mo.

That was it – Miss Zhang had had enough. She told Mr Ma that she would no longer be coming to teach English to his son.

Mo thought about Miss Zhang and her large mouth and her crossness over the questions, and decided that if Uncle Dink hadn't fallen in love with Ms Lin because she was too perfect, he might like Miss Zhang instead.

Mo found Miss Zhang's phone number in his father's address book and picked up his mobile.

"Hi, my name is Mo," he said, when she picked up her phone. That was one English sentence he remembered from his lessons.

"Oh, it's you!" she said, quietly.

Miss Zhang wasn't angry with Mo any more. But she was angry with herself for letting a child upset her.

She knew Mo didn't mean any harm by asking those questions. He was just a curious boy, and it was stupid of her to have felt insulted by him.

"Mo, what can I do for you?" she said, politely.

Mo said, "My father said I should call you. I'd like to ask you some questions please. I'd like to practise asking questions in English."

"What are the questions, Mo?" she replied.

"It's difficult to say on the phone. Could you come to my home and give me another English lesson, please?"

Miss Zhang agreed. As a matter of fact, she liked mischievous Mo, he was a lively boy who liked learning about life. If Mr Ma wanted her to be Mo's English tutor again, she would be.

ENTER, MISS ZHANG

Mo still hadn't quite worked out how he was going to introduce Miss Zhang to Uncle Dink.

"Uncle Dink, can you speak English?" he asked, after he'd put down the phone.

"Of course."

Uncle Dink was surfing the Internet and unwilling to speak.

"Do you know something, Uncle Dink? My father has asked someone to come and teach me English – a teacher called Miss Zhang."

Uncle Dink responded with an "Oh" – and nothing else.

Mo was worried.

"Uncle Dink, could you do me a favour? Could you check whether Miss Zhang is qualified to teach me?"

"That's not necessary, Mo. Anyone who knows more than you is qualified to teach you, and you don't know much English at all!"

"Uncle Dink!" Mo threatened, "You are my FAKE parent; you have to be responsible for me!"

Uncle Dink smiled to himself. But he knew Mo wouldn't stop until he agreed with him.

"OK, how do you think I should check her out?" he sighed.

"You must meet her to see if her appearance is alright, and you must listen to her English to see if it is up to standard."

Uncle Dink longed to laugh, but he didn't want Mo to see that.

The next day, Mo went to visit his grandparents who asked him how Uncle Dink had got on with Ms Lin.

Grandma said, "Last weekend, you said Uncle Dink and Ms Lin went to a pottery-making bar."

Mo nodded, "Yes, they did."

Grandpa was anxious, "Are they going out together again?"

"No."

"Did Ms Lin not like your uncle, or did your uncle not like Ms Lin?"

"Uncle Dink didn't like Ms Lin," said Mo.

"But why?" said Grandma. "You said Ms Lin was the most beautiful woman in the world."

"But Uncle Dink says he doesn't like beautiful women."

Grandma asked Grandpa, "What does he mean, he doesn't like beautiful women?"

Grandma was worried. "Mo, what kind of a woman do you think your uncle will like?"

"I've found someone else for him." Mo struck his chest with his hand to guarantee, "This time Uncle Dink will be satisfied because Miss Zhang is not perfect. She has a big mouth and small eyes."

"Who is Miss Zhang?" enquired Grandma.

95

"Miss Zhang comes to the flat to teach me English. She'll meet Uncle Dink tomorrow."

Grandma was curious about Miss Zhang, and she quite wanted to meet her herself. She said she'd come to Mo's home early next morning and cook a special meal for them.

Mo agreed immediately – he loved Grandma's cooking. She always cooked his favourite things.

On Saturday morning at ten thirty, Miss Zhang arrived and rang the doorbell. She had been expecting to meet Mo's father and was quite surprised to meet a man with brightly coloured hair, and two elderly people.

Mo first introduced Miss Zhang to Uncle Dink, and then to Grandpa and Grandma.

Grandpa and Grandma had never seen a woman with such a big mouth in their whole lives.

"Can he really be interested in someone like that?" said Grandma.

Fortunately Miss Zhang didn't hear Grandma's whisper, she was too busy talking to Uncle Dink in English. "Blah, blah, blah"… Mo and his grandparents couldn't understand a single word.

Uncle Dink and Miss Zhang couldn't stop talking once they started. Mo tried to interrupt them a few

times but he couldn't get a word in edgeways. Still, he didn't mind not having his English lesson, match-making was much more fun.

It was time for lunch. Grandma served her most delicious Korean baked beef with a plate of pea green lettuce, which was used to wrap round the beef.

Uncle Dink picked up some pieces of beef and clumsily wrapped them in the biggest lettuce leaf he could find. The beef ball was as big as a fist.

Uncle Dink handed the fist-sized beef ball with both hands to Miss Zhang. She put the *whole thing* into her mouth without any difficulty.

Mo was shocked. But Uncle Dink seemed very pleased.

Usually Uncle Dink said very little, but today he talked all the time. He talked only to Miss Zhang, and in English.

Mo protested. "Please stop speaking English. Grandpa and Grandma can't understand."

Mo wasn't going to say that he couldn't understand either.

So they spoke politely in Chinese trying to find a suitable topic.

Miss Zhang asked Uncle Dink who his favourite actors were.

Uncle Dink said he really liked Julia Roberts and Hsu Chi. Mo knew these two women actors had ENORMOUS mouths!

Then Uncle Dink asked Miss Zhang what her favourite animals were in the zoo. Miss Zhang laughed, and said they would have to be a Hippopotamus and a Crocodile! Uncle Dink winked. He thought that was very funny.

After Miss Zhang left, Mo asked Grandpa and Grandma what they thought of her.

Grandpa and Grandma were silent for a long time

before Grandma said, "She needs a plastic surgery to make her eyes bigger and her mouth smaller."

"Why?" Uncle Dink asked. "Don't you think she is very beautiful?"

SUCCESS for Mo. His idea was working out!

THE STORM WALKER'S CLUB

Uncle Dink was still living at Mo's flat, even though Mo's parents had returned from their business trip. But if Mo's parents were out, or they went away for the weekend, Uncle Dink would stay in with Mo.

One Friday evening, Uncle Dink suddenly called Mo, saying he wouldn't be back for dinner.

Mo asked, "Then what shall I eat?"

Uncle Dink said, "Just eat some instant noodles."

"I don't want to eat instant noodles." Mo protested. "They give me wind."

Every time Mo ate instant noodles, he always farted. Mo called these farts his "instant farts" and they were really rather smelly.

Uncle Dink told Mo to cook some fried rice and eggs for himself instead.

"Uncle Dink, you're still my fake parent. You are responsible for me when my parents are out. Please come home and have dinner with me."

Uncle Dink gave in, as usual. "OK. Wait in the flat and I'll come and fetch you."

"Fetch me where?" said Mo, curiously.

"That's one question too many!" Uncle Dink was getting irritated with Mo. "You'll find out when we get there."

Mo waited and waited. He was getting hungry and a little bit scared. It was dark by the time Uncle Dink got to the flat.

"Come on then!" Uncle Dink seemed cross. "Remind me never to have a child. Children can be so annoying!"

Mo said, "Well, if you don't become a father then you won't ever be a REAL man." Now Mo was cross.

Uncle Dink took Mo to an area of town he didn't think he should be in. It was known as the Pub Street,

a narrow road honeycombed with dozens of pubs.

They walked into a small pub with a green door and windows, where there were crowds of people. They were all in casual clothes – no suits and no high-heeled shoes. Everyone was chatting or looking at photos displayed on the walls – photos of amazing scenery and people doing outdoor adventurous things

Uncle Dink told Mo that the pub was where the Storm Walkers met.

Mo didn't know what a Storm Walker was.

Uncle Dink said Storm Walkers were groups of people who got together via emails or websites to do completely crazy things. They were people who lived for adventure, travel, and the outdoors. For example they might rush into McDonalds and start dancing a conga there, winding through the tables where people were eating their food. Or they might meet in front of a supermarket shouting "Aliens are coming" three times and then suddenly disappear. Or they might all meet up and climb a mountain, then slide down it on an ironing board.

Uncle Dink said that at weekends and during public holidays, Storm Walkers did crazy things from dawn to night without stopping. But on working days, they did normal jobs. He said the people in the pub were mostly IT professionals like him, or doctors, teachers, engineers and journalists.

"Are there any primary school pupils like me?" asked Mo.

"No," said Uncle Dink firmly. Mo, like sticky toffee, was hard to get rid of once you got involved with him.

"Hello!" Miss Zhang came from nowhere and stood in front of them. "Have you been here ages?" It seemed she had arranged to meet Uncle Dink.

Mo looked at her and then at Uncle Dink and found they both looked a bit soppy.

Mo was beginning to understand something.

"Miss Zhang, are *you* a Storm Walker?"

"You could say that. But your uncle is a Senior Storm Walker."

Why didn't Mo know that? Apparently there were a lot of things about Uncle Dink that Mo did not know.

Miss Zhang asked Uncle Dink, "Where are we

going tomorrow? Have they decided?"

Uncle Dink said, "Curled Dragon Mountain. We climb up the far side of the mountain along the upper reaches of Ya River."

Curled Dragon Mountain was a famous sightseeing place, and Ya River a tributary of the Yangtze River.

"We're setting out at six o'clock tomorrow morning. I've rented a car, got the tent, sleeping bags, food and a safety rope." Uncle Dink said to Miss Zhang, "I'll pick you up early."

"I want to go with you!" Mo yelled. "I've got a tent, and I've been camping before with my friends. We can tell ghost stories!"

"No!" Uncle Dink was determined. "Mo, this is not something for a child. It's exhausting, difficult... and dangerous. You cannot come."

Mo pleaded, "Uncle Dink, are you so cruel as to leave a small child at home alone?"

Mo sounded so pathetic, Miss Zhang was touched. "Let's take Mo with us," she begged.

"But he is so troublesome and mischievous, he'll be a real pain," said Uncle Dink.

"Children are always troublesome. We can take care of him together," said Miss Zhang.

For that single sentence, Mo would give anything now for Miss Zhang to marry his uncle. To Mo, Miss Zhang's mouth didn't look as big as before and her eyes looked wide. In fact she seemed more and more nice-looking.

CRAZY ADVENTURES

It was still dark went they left the city and there weren't many cars on the road. Mo was still quite sleepy – he wasn't used to getting up quite so early. But they arrived at the foot of Curled Dragon Mountain in just under three hours.

Several cars were already at the meeting place when Uncle Dink, Mo and Miss Zhang arrived. When everyone had turned up, the cars were unloaded and walking boots put on.

Uncle Dink carried the tent on his back, rolled up under his backpack. Miss Zhang carried the rolled-up

sleeping bags, and Mo the backpack of food. Uncle Dink told Mo to be careful. "Mo, carrying the food is a big responsibility. We don't want to starve on this trip. And... no eating on the way."

Mo didn't think Uncle Dink was being fair – of course Mo would be careful with the food.

"Taa Raa Taa Raa…"

A man in a red cap blew on a trumpet. He was a famous surgeon and was said to be the most qualified and most experienced Storm Walker in the club. He was chosen to be their guide today.

"Guys, let's go!" he yelled.

They avoided the tourists' mountain path and walked on the rough ground. The Storm Walkers' motto was 'follow your own path, not another's'.

It was very difficult to climb not using the footpath. The earth was covered with thick layers of decayed leaves and tangled roots and tendrils. Mo blundered and tumbled as if someone was deliberately tripping him up.

Uncle Dink kept nagging at him to move faster.

"Mo, hurry up! We're lagging behind the others."

Mo looked ahead. There was a little red spot a long way away up the mountain. It was their guide's red cap.

Mo gasped for breath, "Why are they walking so fast?"

"We must get to the Yangtze River before dark. We will have to walk all night if we go at your speed!" yelled Uncle Dink.

Mo tumbled again. Now there were clumps of snow on the mountainside. Mo slipped and fell into a hole.

Fortunately the hole wasn't very deep. Uncle Dink grabbed Mo's hands, and Miss Zhang helped pull him out.

"It's too dangerous for Mo!" said Miss Zhang. She pointed at a snowdrift nearby and said to Uncle Dink, "If he had stepped there, he would have slid down the cliff."

Uncle Dink tried to find a long stick for Mo so that he could make sure the places he stepped were safe.

"There is a stick hanging on the tree there!" Miss Zhang reached out her hand and pulled the stick and screamed, "Oh, No!"

The "stick" she held turned out to be a frozen snake! It was cold and slippery but was getting warmer in her hands.

Miss Zhang was so scared that she sat on the ground and couldn't move. Mo and Uncle Dink lifted her up and they carried on.

Nothing could stop them. This was a crazy adventure but they weren't going back now. The further they went, the more beautiful the scenery was.

This was the far side of Curled Dragon Mountain. The near side had been developed into a famous sightseeing spot. But these sightseeing spots were always crowded with tourists, hotels, peddlars selling trinkets, and sedan-chair lifters who pestered tourists to ride in their chairs.

At the far side of Curled Dragon Mountain, the mountain was too high and the water was too deep. That's why it had not been developed and opened to the tourists. Only the adventurous Storm Walker who didn't want to follow another's path had the chance to enjoy the stunning scenery.

"Hi, Dink...Dink...Dink..."

There were echoes among the hills. Their guide was calling them.

"Uncle Dink. We're about to catch up with them!" yelled Mo, excitedly.

"It's too early to say that," said Uncle Dink, "They're on a different peak. We have to go round the river valley to meet them."

Though the valley wasn't very wide, it would take a

long time to go round it to get to the other side. How Mo wished he had a propeller on his back like a helicopter or had wings for arms so that he could fly over.

Uncle Dink was thinking the same thing. He saw a tree stretching out over the valley.

"Mo, do you want to fly across the valley?"

Of course Mo did. By doing that, he wouldn't have so far to walk and he could catch up with the guide in the red cap.

"But how can I fly without propeller and wings?"

Uncle Dink said, "With this."

He took out a safety rope from his backpack, which had a claw at one end. Uncle Dink threw the hook over to the tree stretching out over the valley. The claw held firmly.

Uncle Dink pulled the safety rope two or three times. It was safe.

"We can swing over using the rope, like Tarzan in the jungle," he said.

Uncle Dink grabbed hold over the rope, swung easily to the other side of the valley and then back again – it looked so easy.

Uncle Dink asked Miss Zhang and Mo, "Who wants to go first?"

Both Miss Zhang and Mo wanted to.

Uncle Dink said, "Ladies first."

Miss Zhang grabbed the rope, lifted up her feet and swung over the valley. She jumped off the other side and threw the end of the rope back to the others.

Then it was Mo's turn.

Uncle Dink handed the end of the rope to him and told him to grab it firmly with both hands. He said to Mo, "Don't look down, close your eyes. It won't take long."

Disobeying Uncle Dink's order, Mo opened his eyes and looked down. He saw white torrents beneath. This was even more exciting than bungee jumping; he felt like Tarzan in the jungle, leaping between trees. But it was soon over and Mo was safely on the other side.

Miss Zhang threw the end of the rope back to Uncle Dink and soon all three of them were on the right side of the valley to catch up with the rest of the group.

When they joined the other Storm Walkers, they all decided it was time to eat their food, and drink some water from a mountain spring.

"Mo, where is our food?" asked Uncle Dink.

Mo had nothing with him. Before swinging across the valley, he'd put the food pack, which seemed heavy, on the ground... and left it there. Now he was on one side of the valley, and the food bag was on the other.

"Oh Mo, Mo. You are HOPELESS," said Uncle Dink.

The other Storm Walkers' felt sorry for them and shared some of their food – after all, they couldn't let a sweet little child starve, could they?

SPIDERMAN ON THE CLIFF

They didn't have long before the guide made them get going again. They crossed to another section of the mountain and saw a mighty river, pouring down and running away.

"Ya River! Ya River!" They shouted and jumped for joy.

With a cliff above it and torrents beneath, the path along the Ya River was even more dangerous.

The guide looked at the landscape through his

binoculars. "Please prepare the safety rope. We'll have to climb the cliff."

Climbing a cliff was quite different from climbing up the mountain. You only had to use your feet to walk up a mountain – however steep – but to climb the cliff, you had to use both your hands as well! You had to attach your body to the cliff and move upwards along a safety rope, like a spider attached to the wall.

"This will be a real test!" said the guide. "This is the most dangerous part of our journey. It will be a test for our team work and our bravery. We must take good care of ourselves, especially the child. I'll go first and Dink can bring up the rear."

"No. I'll go first and you bring up the rear," said Dink.

It was more dangerous to go first. But Uncle Dink had won a cliff-climbing race the previous year and was nicknamed "Spiderman". The group leader agreed that Dink should go first.

Uncle Dink hugged the cliff with his body, then moved upwards using his hands and feet, fastening the rope's claw to places that were safe and firm. Then everyone behind Uncle Dink held on to the safety rope and followed him up.

Mo was right behind Miss Zhang, who was right behind Uncle Dink. Mo's feet trembled when he took the first few steps and Miss Zhang told him to hang on to her waist.

"Mo, are you afraid?" asked Miss Zhang gently.

Mo didn't reply. "Are you?"

"No. I'm not afraid as long as I have your Uncle Dink nearby," she whispered.

Mo said immediately, "I'm not afraid as long as I have *you* nearby."

Having Spiderman Dink as their leader the little team moved along the cliff quickly and smoothly.

The river became wider and wider and the mist in the hills cleared up. They even saw a scarlet ray of sunlight on the horizon.

They all got excited because they knew their destination was close. The next bit of the path was easier. They didn't need Uncle Dink to lead, or the safety rope any more.

But Uncle Dink had slowed down, and so had Miss Zhang. They were picking something up from the ground.

"What are you doing?" asked Mo.

"We're collecting a kind of wild plant – it's called mugwort," said Miss Zhang. "We'll make some soup with it later."

The river became wider and shallower. Shoals of fish were swimming in the water.

"Mo, do you want to eat baked fish?" asked Uncle Dink.

 117

What was his uncle thinking of! They didn't have a fishing rod!

Mo hadn't noticed a black plastic bag hooked under Uncle Dink's backpack. The black bag was filled with different white plastic bags and empty mineral water bottles. Mo didn't remember seeing Uncle Dink with these things when they started out.

"Didn't you see me collecting these things along the way?" said Uncle Dink.

Mo was confused. Why had Uncle Dink been collecting rubbish?

Miss Zhang said, "Your Uncle is being green."

Mo knew his uncle had colourful hair, but he hadn't noticed that he was *green*. What did Miss Zhang mean?

Miss Zhang said, "What I mean is that your uncle is an environmentalist. He likes to care for the environment. We must do the same, Mo."

So his Uncle Dink was a brand new human, and also an environmentalist.

Uncle Dink chose a couple of the big plastic bags and made some little holes in them with his knife. These would be his fishing nets!

Uncle Dink took off his shoes and socks, stood in

118

the river with bare feet, opened a bag and put it into the river.

The river flowed into the bag and with it came several fish. Uncle Dink gently lifted the bag and three wriggling fish were left in the bag once the water had flowed out.

"I want to go fishing too," laughed Mo.

Mo took off his shoes and socks and stepped into the river. The water was absolutely freezing! Mo shivered, but went to fish with his uncle.

Soon Uncle Dink and Mo had caught over twenty fish, enough for everyone. Miss Zhang had collected a big bag of plants to make a huge pot of soup.

At sunset, the Storm Walkers finally saw the Yangtze River. They settled on a wide and flat riverbank. Tents in various colours were pitched, and the campfire was lit. The men baked the fish in the fire, and the women made soup with water from the river and the plants they'd collected. Only Mo had nothing to do. He didn't think he could boss all these Storm Walkers round like he had with his friends once, at a school barbecue.

They all sat around the campfire and ate fresh and delicious baked fish with wild plant soup that tasted

a little bitter. Mo looked at Uncle Dink, who was devouring the fish and sweating heavily. He couldn't believe that this was the same man who worked on his laptop in the café, ate just a small sandwich for lunch and drank double-shot lattes with a dash of vanilla.

If this is what being a brand new human really was, Mo couldn't wait to grow up.

But if Uncle Dink married Miss Zhang, Mo wanted to stay a child, *their* child – if only for a weekend!

READER'S NOTE

MO'S WORLD

Mo Shen Ma lives in a big city in China. Modern Chinese cities are very much like ours, so his life is not so different from your own: he goes to school, watches television and gets into mischief – just like kids all over the world!

There are some differences, though. Chinese writing is completely unlike our own. There is no alphabet, and words are not made up of letters – instead, each word is represented by a little drawing called a character. For us, learning to read is easy. There are only twenty-six letters that make up all our words! But in Chinese, every word has its own character. Even Simplified Chinese writing uses a basis of 6,800 different characters. Each character has to be learned by heart, which means that it takes many years for a Chinese student to learn to read fluently.

NAMES

Chinese personal names carry various meanings, and the names in this book have definitely been chosen for a reason! Take Mo Shen Ma, the hero of our tale. His name is made up of the words Mo, which means "good ideas", and Shen, which means "deep" or "profound". So you can see how much his name suits him, because Mo Shen is always coming up with great ideas!

STORY BACKGROUND

In this story, Mo hikes along the Yangtze River with his uncle Dink and the rest of the Storm Walkers. The Yangtze River is 6300 kilometres in length. It is the longest river in Asia and the third longest river in the world. Mo and his uncle climbed the mountains near the Ya River – one of more than 700 tributaries or streams that feed into the Yangtze River.

The word Yangtze comes from the name "Yang", a lord who ruled a region of China in ancient times. And although we refer to this river as the Yangtze here, in China the river is called Chang Jiang, or "Long River". It is also sometimes called Da Jiang, "Great River" or simply Jiang, which means "River".

The Yangtze is the most important river in China. It is a major source of water for farming and supplying energy. Nearly one third of China's population lives in the river

region. It is also a beautiful destination for nature lovers. You can see why Mo's Uncle Dink was trying to make sure the river and surrounding mountain area were kept clean.

Hiking with Uncle Dink reminds Mo about his barbecue. You can read about it in *Teacher's Pet*. And in *Four Troublemakers*, Mo and his friends, Hippo, Penguin, and Monkey camp out in a tent. They have a hilarious time scaring each other with spooky stories!

Meet the mischievous star of China's favourite series!

Name: Mo Shen Ma

Likes: Mischief

Dislikes: Homework.

Latest Mischief: Getting together with his friends
Hippo, Penguin and Monkey to play at being
superheroes! But Mo and his friends only have one
superpower: getting into trouble...

Meet the mischievous star of China's favourite series!

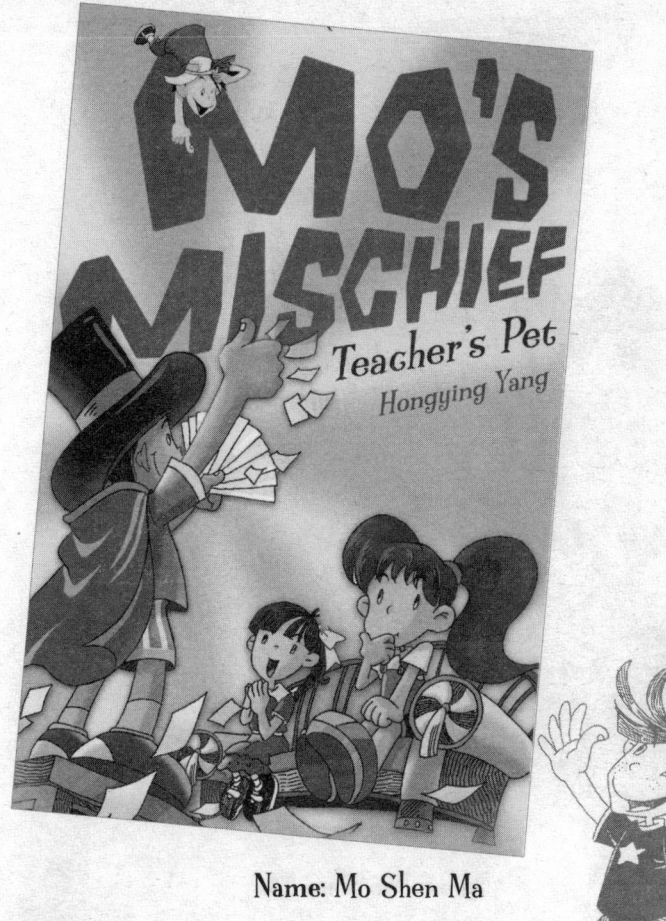

Name: Mo Shen Ma

Likes: Mischief

Dislikes: Homework.

Latest Mischief: Being really nice to Lu, the class goody-goody. Giving her flowers when she gets ill. But Mo hates Lu. He must be up to something...

Meet the mischievous star of China's favourite series!

Name: Mo Shen Ma

Likes: Mischief

Dislikes: Homework.

Latest Mischief: Going to his grandma's house for the summer holidays and teaching Grandma's pig to roller-skate! But Mo hadn't reckoned on the monkeys being as mischievous as he is...

Meet the mischievous star of China's favourite series!

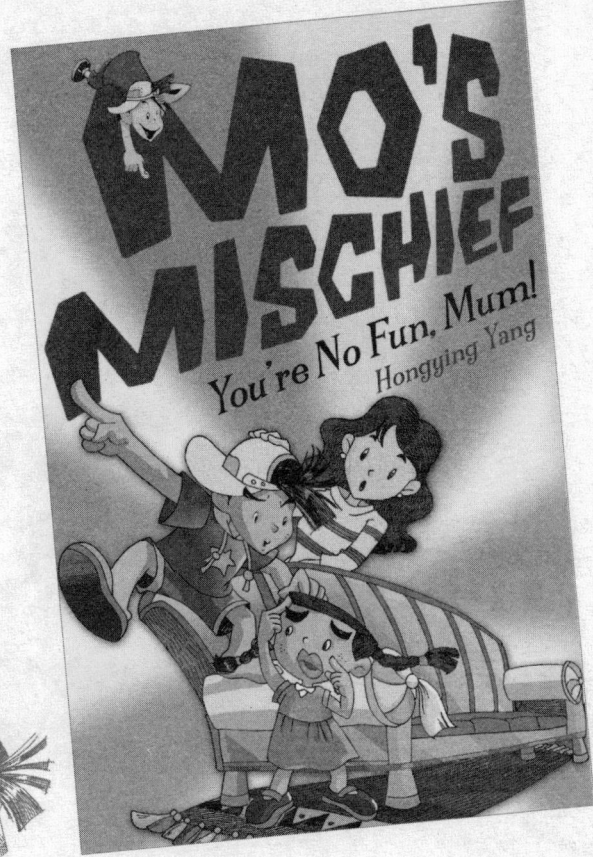

Name: Mo Shen Ma

Likes: Mischief

Dislikes: Homework.

Latest Mischief: Framing his Dad for one of his own practical jokes - and getting caught by Mum! It seems like whenever Mo plans a trick, his mum is always there to stop him. Can Mo beat her and have some real fun?

Meet the mischievous star of China's favourite series!

MO'S MISCHIEF
Best Friends
Hongying Yang

Name: Mo Shen Ma

Likes: Mischief

Dislikes: Homework.

Latest Mischief: Hanging around with the prettiest girl in school. But hasn't Mo learned his lesson? Talking to girls always leads to trouble...!